atheneum

ATHENEUM BOOKS FOR YOUNG READERS
An imprint of Simon & Schuster Children's Publishing Division
1230 Avenue of the Americas, New York, New York 10020
For information about special discounts for bulk purchases, please contact Simon & Schuster Special Sales
at 1-866-506-1949 or business@simonandschuster.com.
The Simon & Schuster Speakers Bureau can bring authors to your live event. For more
information or to book an event, contact the Simon & Schuster Speakers Bureau at
1-866-248-3049 or visit our website at www.simonspeakers.com.
Book design by Sonia Chaghatzbanian
The text for this book is hand-lettered.
The illustrations for this book are rendered in watercolor.
Manufactured in China
0415 SCP
6 8 10 9 7
Library of Congress Cataloging-in-Publication Data
Campbell, Scott, 1973- author, illustrator.
Hug machine / by Scott Campbell.
p. cm.
Summary: The Hug Machine is available to hug anyone, any time,
whether they are square or long, spiky or soft.
ISBN 978-1-4424-5935-9 (hardcover)
ISBN 978-1-4424-5936-6 (eBook)
[1. Hugging—Fiction.] I. Title.
PZ7.C1583Hug 2014
[E]—dc23   2013019664

HUG
MACHINE

By Scott Campbell

Atheneum Books for Young Readers
New York London Toronto Sydney New Delhi

Whoa!

Here I come!

I am the Hug Machine!

I am very good at hugging.

The best at hugging.

No one can resist my unbelievable hugging.

I am the Hug Machine!

My hugs calm people down.

They cheer them up.

They make them go completely nuts!

I am the Hug Machine!

I hug everything I see!

No one escapes the Hug Machine.

My hugs make the biggest feel small.

The smallest feel big.

I hug soft things.

Hard things.

Square things.

Long things!

I am the Hug Machine!

Oh.
Do you need a hug?

I think you do.

HUG ACCOMPLISHED!

There is nothing the Hug Machine will not hug.

"What about me? I am so spiky. No one ever hugs me."

"What about me? Surely I am too big for you to hug."

Not for the Hug Machine!

People often ask what the Hug Machine eats to keep the hugging energy high.

Well, the answer is pizza.
The Hug Machine likes pizza very much.

Whew! What a tiring day of hugging.
The Hug Machine is exhausted.

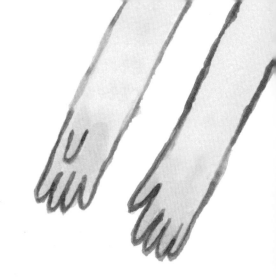

Hug Machine can hug no more.

Oh.

Why, yes. **You** may hug the Hug Machine.

Hug Machine is always open for business.

Hug Checklist